CW00384338

THE KAMA SUITE

An Anthology of Premiered Stories for Alpha Men

Margareth Moore

TABLE OF CONTENTS

VIXEN THE FOX

Christian came home after a long day at work and wanted to relax and forget the day. It had been a particularly stressful time for a lawyer who was in court for a week.

He went through the front door of his apartment with a panoramic view of the city and threw off his shoes. As he looked around, he noticed that something was wrong.

There was a bowl of water on the floor, and water was splashing around it. Crumbs on the floor. Paperwork had been spread out as if someone had been digging through it. At first Christian was worried that there had been a break-in, but nothing seemed to be missing. Then he heard scratching from the other room and smiled.

Vixen was here.

Vixen, known in her "normal" life as Jane, was Christian's lover. She was more than that. She was his little girl. She was completely devoted to him. But today, she was Vixen. She loved to play house as his pet.

Still in his suit, Christian entered the bedroom and found Vixen in her fox ears and tail. The tail was secured by a plug in her tight little bottom. She looked up at him with a stubborn look and went back to her snack, a little tartlet that she ate without hands. Her bottom was wiggling, her tail was wagging.

"Vixen? Come here, baby," said Christian.

She did not answer.

Foxes often didn't answer.

The way she dealt with foxes-was different from other pets. Kittens were cute and sometimes a bit independent. Puppies were always by her side. But foxes were very different. They were mischievous, playful and naughty.

"Fox?" he said again, but she didn't answer again. He began to approach her, and she grabbed the muffin in her mouth and began to run on all fours, trying to get past him.

She scurried into the living room and he followed her. At that point, everything was carefree. Vixen often made Christian chase her. He could have been her master, but she was mischievous and liked to hunt.

He cornered her in the living room while the half-eaten cupcake was still in her mouth. They were next to the big window, which reached from floor to ceiling and gave a view of the city.

"Good girl. Put the snack down and come over to Daddy," said Christian.

The fox felt obedient and did as she was told. She looked up at his eyes while he looked down. Silently, he began stroking her hair and playing with her ears. Her beautiful body could be seen in front of him.

"Good girl. Help Daddy out," said Christian.

Christian unzipped his trousers while his suit was still on. He pulled out his tail, which was already half hard, and came closer. Smiling, Vixen took it in her mouth.

At first it was just the head of his cock. It began to grow in her mouth. She felt it pulsating. The stress of the day immediately left Christian's face.

"Mmmmm. What a good girl." He said as she started to push him further, his cock got wet from her mouth and started to act on him. He was now completely hard and buried in his pet's mouth.

He wrapped his hand in her hair, guided her mouth, but let Vixen choose how she wanted to satisfy him. His hand continued to caress her.

As he quickly approached orgasm, he stopped her. He didn't want to end up in his pet's mouth today, although Vixen would have liked to please him that way.

"Vixen, get on the couch." He said to her. Pets were never allowed on the furniture without permission. Her eyes sparkled as she let his tail pop out of her mouth, and she walked towards the couch. She looked at him and smiled and ran off on all fours.

"Vixen!" he said loud and stern. But she was in her own little world and she ran. She went into the guest room to hide from him. He found her quickly on the floor between the bed and the wall. She looked up at him, knowing that she had been disobedient, but she didn't care.

Not knowing where to go, she looked at him with big eyes.

"On the bed." He said, without the carefree tone that he had had before.

She obeyed.

On the bed, on all fours, Vixen was a sight to behold. She was naked to her ears and the tip of her tail. Her beautiful breasts hanging full and firm. ...her bottom sticking out and looking so inviting. Inviting enough that Christian couldn't help himself.

SMACK

His hand found her ass, punishment for her disobedience.

"Aren't you listening to me anymore?" he asked. Her eyes smiled. While the beating hurt, it was what she longed for.

SMACK.

His hand found her ass again and left a distinct mark. She squawked with reaction. The pain was intense, but her pussy got wetter and wetter.

SMACK.

He reconnected with her. She resisted. The shock went through her body.

He grabbed her ass with his hands and positioned her on the edge of the bed. He was still wearing his work clothes, with his now completely hard cock exposed. He stood behind her. He pressed his erection against her soft lips.

"Do you want me inside you, vixen?" he asked. Her protests melted away and she pushed back against him, the only answer she could think of.

His tail pressed past her lips and slowly he began to stretch them. He could feel her wetness enveloping him. Again she began to whimper as he pushed her further. Her soft cock tickled him when he was finally completely inside his little pet.

"Fuck baby, you're so tight." He told her. That made her smile and wiggle her ass even more.

The wiggling and the tightness of her ass almost made Christian obsessed. He pushed inside her and started fucking his pet. His body slammed into hers.

"Ungh... Ungh... ...ungh..." She moaned and grunted with every stitch. Pets didn't talk.

"Play with your clitoris, vixen." He said to her. It was an order, not a suggestion.

Vixen did as she was told and reached down and played with her clitoris while he punched his pet. At that moment, she was his, and she lived to please him. Her bratty, foxy nature was almost forgotten.

As he punched her and occasionally slapped her backside again to remind her who was in control, her moans grew louder.

Suddenly he pulled away from her. She whimpered and wanted to get fed again. He turned her around forcibly and threw himself back into her wet pussy. She screamed. The desire increased.

"Did I tell you to stop playing with your clitoris?" he asked.

Quickly she put her fingers back on the button and pressed herself closer to him. She was on display for him. Her legs were spread at the end of the bed, her tail hanging down. He could see the plug buried in her asshole.

She began to tremble. Once again her squeaking and moaning became more urgent. Her body began to tense up.a

"Go ahead, honey, you can cum for me."

That was all she needed. She tipped over the edge and screamed as the orgasm flowed through her body.

"Good girl, come for Daddy. That's a good girl." That was all he could say as he struggled against his own pleasure.

He stopped, his dick all buried in his pet. Her orgasm settled and her body stopped shaking.

He pulled himself out of her.

Christian knelt on the floor and kissed her pussy. He tasted his beautiful pet.

Then Vixen felt pressure. She got the plug pulled. Christian slowly pulled it out of her asshole. She felt a rush as the big plug was removed from her ass. That opened her up to him.

Vixen felt a warm fluid at her narrow opening. Christian lubricated her, and she knew what that meant. Her body temporarily cramped up. Christian lubricated his own cock into the lubricant, which was already wet with her sperm.

While she was still lying on her back, he pushed her legs up. Her eyes were big when she looked at him.

The hard head of his cock pressed against her tight ring. It was firm but gentle. Eventually her tension gave way and he slowly penetrated her.

"Oh, Daddy!" she said as he grabbed her ass. The talking was against the rules, but Christian did not want to punish his pet for this little transgression.

His dick slid slowly into her until he grabbed her ass. She moaned uncontrollably. Slowly, he began to caress her. She felt an incredible mixture of pleasure and pain. She gave way to an almost complete pleasure.

Gently he worked his way out of her and back in, slipped in and fucked her tight asshole. He now moaned audibly, unable to control his own pleasure. Her tight ass grabbed him.

"Shit, good girl." That was all he could say.

"Baby, Vixen, I'll be right there."

And she moaned.

"Oh, baby..." His voice faded. He pushed himself all the way into her and emptied himself, filled her tight orifice with his semen. He stayed inside her and watched her eyes roll and she squirm.

"Good girl," he said as he allowed himself to come out of her. He could see his sperm dripping out of her.

Still in his suit, he fell beside her. He pulled her towards him and kissed her deeply.

"My good girl."

THE EDGE

It had been two weeks since Daddy had his princess hosed down. She was now tied up on his bed and waiting.

Her wrists were tied and fastened to the posts of the bed. There was not enough room to even allow her to touch herself. Her legs were bound, bent at the knee and spread. She was fully exposed to him. A blindfold prevented her from seeing what was going on in the room.

Before that, the princess had proved that she was capable of going a week without orgasm. She was irritable every day. At least thirty minutes a day. But at least once she stood for three hours before the abyss. She had been a soaking wet mess.

Towards the end, she could hardly think anymore. Her thoughts were confused. She could not answer her father clearly. It was as if she was intoxicated. It was only a week ago.

This week ended with a shuddering orgasm that left her screaming and shaking. It had been worth it. Her daddy was proud. But then he said those words.

"Good girl. I think my princess can probably last two weeks."

Those words seemed to resonate. And her daddy meant it. After her shaking from orgasm, he told her, "Princess, I hope you enjoyed that, it's the last orgasm you'll have for two weeks. Longer if you don't obey."

She whimpered as he put his dick to her lips. Obedient, she took it in her mouth like a good girl. He ended up on her chest

and covered her with his sperm. Like an obedient little girl, she rubbed it on and wallowed in the feeling that Daddy's semen was covering her.

For the next thirteen days she was tortured. She was not allowed to touch herself at all without Daddy's knowledge and consent. Even washing her kitten required Daddy's consent. Daddy always gave her permission for the most necessary things, but she knew that he loved to have the power to refuse her if he wanted to.

On the first day, the princess had forgotten to load her toy properly so she could not give in to Daddy's instructions. She felt the familiar sting of worry when she told him about it. He was not worried and continued her delicious game for about an hour. She came four times just before orgasm, but she was a good princess and kept herself from tipping.

Only after her playing session on the first day did he tell her that she should be punished for her transgression. She was told to put a drop of the peppermint oil she had in her cabinet on her sensitive clitoris after playing for an hour. Then she was allowed to squirm and moan, as daddy did not allow her to touch or rub it. She was forced to re-apply it halfway through. Only after a quarter of an hour she was allowed to touch herself and get some relief. He enjoyed her moaning and groaning and crying.

On her third day she begged to be allowed to cum. Only three days inside. Daddy didn't like that. The princess was told to stop touching herself immediately. She obeyed. She almost

always obeyed. Then she was told to take her harvest from the drawer. Nervously, she agreed.

"Five sharp blows to the clitoris. Is that clear?" He demanded.

"Yes, Daddy." She answered quietly.

The sharp pain gave way to pleasure. By the fifth slap, she was afraid she was gonna come. She held back.

"Now do it again, and remember, you shouldn't beg unless you mean it." He said stern.

"Oh fuck Daddy, it hurts and it feels so good." She moaned and whimpered. Daddy smiled.

At the end of the session, the princess was left panting and shivering, desperately seeking relief that Daddy didn't want to give her.

Several days passed and the princess became nervous. She used toys on her clitoris and inside, as Daddy had told her to. She was a good princess.

On the eighth day, which was now the longest day she had ever gone without an orgasm, the princess received an instruction from Daddy.

"Today, after you shower, you are to insert a butt plug You will not remove it until I tell you to."

She blanched. That would mean the princess would have to wear her butt plug all day long. She chose a dress and panties. She hardly ever wore panties with a dress, but she was

worried about the toys that would be inside. She didn't want it to fall out, even though she knew that because of its design this would not happen. With some lubricant and her leg on the counter, Princess pushed the plug into herself. She moaned loudly as it was pushed past her tight ring. Every step and bump in the car that day reminded her of Daddy's control. She loved the feeling.

When she came home that day, Daddy was waiting for her.

"How does it feel, princess?" he asked.

"Full of Daddy, so full. I'm dripping."

He lifted the dress over her head and took off her bra. He pushed her face down on the bed. Then he turned on the vibration. The plug that had lain dormant in her tight ass came to life. The princess could feel the vibrations inside her.

Daddy reached under her and played with her clitoris. This was the first time in two weeks that Daddy was the one who turned her on. Without her own hand controlling the touches, she was afraid she would fall over the edge.

Daddy pushed one, then two fingers into her wet hole.

"Princess, you're so wet."

"Yes, Daddy!" That was all she could say.

With his fingers inside her, he started playing with his thumb on her clitoris. The feeling was almost overwhelming. Her whole body was shaking.

"Please, Daddy! Daddy. Please, Daddy, please. "Her plea became almost incomprehensible: "If... ...not... ...stop... ...jerk off." She gasped.

That's when Daddy turned everything off. She moaned and whimpered.

"Daddy wants to fuck your tits, princess."

"Yes, Daddy, play with your toys." And the princess said.

Daddy smiled and turned them over. He spread her chest and put his cock between her tits. Like a good girl, she pushed them together and he began to caress them. He grabbed a bottle of oil that was on the bedside table and rubbed himself with it. He stroked it again and began to moan.

"Oh fuck, princess, it feels so good to have Daddy coming."

"Yes, Daddy, please, please, please come all over your toys. Cover my tits, Daddy." She said enthusiastically. With that, he pushed himself over the top and ropes of semen broke out of his twitchy dick over her tits.

"Good girl," he said as he cuddled her, still covered with his sperm, and they fell asleep together, the princess longing for more.

Day twelve was the hardest of all. The princess had no responsibilities, and Dad, although he was at work, was determined to give her an advantage all day long. The first rule of the day was that she was not to wear any clothes at all from waking until going to bed. Nothing. And the second rule

was that whenever Papa asked her to, she had to exert herself for at least thirty minutes to get as close to orgasm as possible.

It started at 6:30 in the morning. The princess was awakened by the sound of her telephone alarm.

The text only said, "Fuck you, princess."

She took out her glass dildo and put it inside her, slowly, while her eyes opened from sleep, she pushed it in and out. It took her about ten minutes to see the other line.

"Put a vibrator on your clitoris. Leave it on there until you can no longer hold yourself back. It must be on high."

When the impulses started, it jerked involuntarily. The dildo was still pressing into her and she moaned as she resisted the feeling. She was proud when she was constantly stimulated for 20 minutes. In the past two weeks she had learned how to push herself as far as she could. The timer was ticking. 22 minutes. She was soaking wet. 24 minutes. Her body began to shake, but she held on. 28 minutes. She was on the edge of the abyss. For two delicious, agonising minutes, she rode on that ridge before putting the toy down. She was exhausted.

At lunchtime, she was instructed to use her magic wand, which was attached to her belt so that it could stay still and was pressed against her clitoris. She had the house to herself and moaned audibly within 5 minutes. She was afraid that she would keel over without permission. The princess almost texted Daddy to ask him to let her cum, but she knew that this would prolong her torture. After fifteen minutes she had to turn it off.

Finally Daddy was home. She had been instructed to be on all fours in the bedroom with no clothes on. She had been instructed not to look back at Daddy.

Daddy entered the room and saw his princess, as he had ordered. Her wet kitten was open and dripping practically. Without saying a word, he undressed and lay down on the bed behind her. At first she felt the pressure, then she noticed that he pushed himself into her. She emitted a throaty moan.

"Oh Daddy!" was all she could say.

"You know, princess, you mustn't come, no matter what happens."

Again she moaned with pleasure and uncertainty.

Slowly, Daddy started fucking his princess. He pushed himself all the way in and let his dick feel her depths. Then he pulled back until the head of his cock spread her lips. Without warning, he slammed it back into her.

"Unnnnnnnngh," she grunted. She could almost see stars when he took control of her and started fucking her. She knew she wasn't allowed to cum, and at that point she knew Daddy would do it. The only question was whether she could outlive him.

When he fucked her mercilessly, she felt his hand on her ass. She hadn't done anything wrong, it was just Daddy enjoying his toys. He loved to mix pain with her pleasure. He knew she loved it too.

"Thank you, Daddy!" She whimpered, almost automatically.

He smiled. What a good princess she was.

She began to tremble. She struggled. He could feel her body fighting the tremor of orgasm. She also knew she couldn't tell him to stop just to avoid an orgasm. It wasn't like she was playing with her toys.

His breathing accelerated and his body became rigid.

"Fuck the baby. Princess". I'm coming!" He growled.

"In me, please, in me, Daddy! Fill your princess up. I need Daddy's sperm!"

And with that he was pushed over the top and filled her tight pussy with his sperm. Exhausted, he stayed there, tucked his cock inside her. Finally it came out of her. She whimpered.

He fell beside her and pulled her inside. "You are perfect, princess," he said to her.

And then it was the 14th day. She had looked forward to that day. But now that she was about to cum, she almost wanted it to last longer.

He had tied her to the bed. Her wrists in handcuffs, her legs tied and spread so that she was on display for him. Her eyes were blindfolded.

"Princess, you may cum today, but only if I allow it." He said with a smile in his voice.

But that was not the deal! She should be able to come today, no matter what She protested almost vociferously, but decided against it.

With spread legs she felt his hot breath on her thighs. Then there was a gentle kiss. On the inside of her thigh she was only a few inches away from her pussy, then she felt his tongue. Dad only licked the outside of her lips, stopped kissing her from time to time, but never came in contact with her pussy, which she needed so desperately.

"Daddy!" was all she said.

He was licking right underneath her opening where her wetness had collected. He loved her taste. Then his tongue began to flutter around her perfect lips.

"Oh, Daddy, thank you!" She squealed. She wasn't allowed to cum yet, but that contact on her pussy was something she desperately needed.

And then she felt his tongue pressing down into her. Her tight wet hole finally got the attention it needed. Even with the blindfold on, she could see colors.

"Do you need Daddy to lick your clitoris?" he asked.

"Oh please, yes please Daddy, please!" She begged.

His tongue found her button and she moaned. He teased her just for a minute because he didn't want her to cum without his cock in her. When he stopped, she screamed.

"No, Daddy, no, don't stop, please!" It was more than just whining. She begged him. She was desperate. She couldn't put a single thought together.

She could feel his weight leaving the bed.

It was nothing.

Five minutes.

Five minutes. Nothing.

She moaned and shouted to him.

She moaned and shouted to him. Nothing.

Ten minutes.

Dripping.

Then she felt something on her clitoris, and before she could react, the wand was raised.

"Oh fuck!" She screamed. Immediately she was on the edge and the toy was pressed against her most sensitive part.

"Oh daddy!" She screamed.

"You better not come." That's all he said. He pushed the toy relentlessly against her.

"Hell, I can't even cum on Daddy," was her unintelligible mumbling.

"I can't stop, I'm gonna..." That was the end of the toy.

She had never come that close to orgasm only to deny it. Her fists were tight balls when she resisted the pleasure. Her pussy just licked when she lay there.

Then she felt his weight again. She didn't dare speak up.

Then his cock pressed against her. Slowly he filled her up. She moaned over her pleasure.

He pushed her in and out. She could hear her wetness sloshing as he fucked her. He held her shoulders down so she couldn't move. She loved his strength.

Then the light hit her face. He had taken off her blindfold. She was staring into his eyes. She was crazy. She couldn't concentrate or think. The joy overwhelmed her.

He put his hand on her throat and squeezed it tight.

"Sperm for me, Princess."

The waves of lust overwhelmed her. She was dizzy. She could only see shapes as the orgasm washed over her. Daddy could feel her pussy tightening around him, and with that he let go and filled his naughty little princess

"Good girl. That's a good girl. What a perfect princess," he murmured in her ear.

When he recovered, he untied her bonds so that they could hold each other.

"That was perfect." She said to him.

He kissed her deep. Together, they slept a satisfying sleep.

SPANKING AND SUBMISSION

I want to be above his knees, the firm warmth of his legs below me. I want to feel close to him, I want to feel him surrounding me. I want to close my eyes and feel my body relax and melt in his lap because I know that this is a safe place.

The touch of his fingers on my skin makes my heart beat with anticipation. I feel the excitement sweeping over me, my whole body tingling with anticipation because I know there is more to come. When he runs his hands over my skin, I sometimes think that I would purr if I could, trapped in the hedonistic joy of it all.

Once he sounded almost amused when he noticed, "You just want to be touched, don't you?" as I arched and trembled and pulled on my shackles to follow his hand that made its way through my neck and along my collarbone. Wherever he touches me, I feel open to give him access, pulling my head back to expose my neck and inviting him to put his hand around my neck.

It must be such a power trip for him that the slightest touch triggers this kind of reaction in me. When he grabs my neck, my whole body remains calm and relaxed, the tensions dissolve and are replaced by the feeling of security and safety. There is always something gentle about his touch, even if it is firm. It sounds strange to say, but even his strokes feel tender in a certain way. Certainly not soft, but the opposite of hard or cruel.

When he caresses my bottom, I bite back my moans. I arch my back and stick out my bottom and do everything I can to make it an invitation.

When his hand comes hard on my butt, I can't stop the moaning and whimpering that slides from my lips. I want to beg, implore him, please, more. Each blow sends a jolt of joy through me. The longer he spanks me, the more I feel the pleasure building up - on what, I'm not sure. All I know is that I'm desperate. I never want him to stop. It's ecstasy.

I'm holding back. I wonder if he knows what he's making me feel. Can he tell how wet I am from the first moment he touches me? That every little touch causes a tingling and a heat flash between my legs? Does he know that my moaning is one of those pleasures? Does he know that I hold back and resist the urge to rub against him? Does he have any idea of the effect he has on me?

I do not ask him to touch me in this way, but I wonder if this thought has crossed his mind. I wonder if he is also holding back.

During our last scene there was a moment when he came up behind me and wordlessly pressed himself against me and let me feel the effect I had on him. It was not a request or demand. There was no expectation. He just showed it to me and shared it with me. This is one of the moments I think back to most later, when I am alone, the memory that makes my toes bend and tremble.

I also remember his hand around my throat, another wordless gesture. He did not press - he did not have to. I closed my

throat, offered him my complete vulnerability and showed him my submission. And he showed me that he was not afraid of it, that he felt and wanted this dominance. He claimed the submission I offered him.

It was a reminder of my physical vulnerability. He is not usually physically intrusive, but he has a quiet strength in himself and I am quite small. His grip around my throat reminds me of this, makes me sharply aware of it. It is the feeling that he could do anything he wants with me, but I still feel safe. When he presses me against a solid surface or holds me down, he doesn't want to defend himself. Through his strength I feel safe in my place there and have confidence that he will take command. I love to submit myself to that.

There are other feelings that I do not put into words for him and which I hope to convey to him by showing them to him. I wonder if he can feel them. I lack the words to say "thank you" to him for what he gives me, how happy I feel to be able to give him my submission. I wish I could make him feel the gratitude that swells in my chest, a different kind of warmth, and I hope he can feel the trust and respect and awe that overwhelms me in these moments. When these feelings overwhelm me, I want to kneel down before him to show him what I cannot express otherwise.

THE STRANGER

One evening, many years ago, I came back from a club whose name I can't remember, but it was in London. I was on a tube train, and there were not too many people on the train; it was late.

I sat and minded my own business. I think it was autumn, because I can't remember it being cold, as was the custom on the train at the time. Somewhere down in the car I noticed a man sitting alone. He looked up and looked me straight in the eye. He had the kind of piercing eyes you just can't look away from. Before I knew it, he had sat down next to me, put his arm around me and started to kiss me with great passion. Wow! I remember that he was dark, maybe Greek, and very handsome. Then he started to put his hand inside my coat. I was so stunned that I just couldn't speak.

I was numb, he was so passionate, and my body reacted immediately. I kept saying to myself: Emily, tell him to move away, but I didn't.

He turned me over, opened my shirt and began to caress my breasts. He whispered in my ear, "I want to fuck you hard."

What shocked me most was my body's reaction to a total stranger. I can't have been more than about 19. Of course I was sexually active and had a boyfriend, so I kept wondering what that was. It turned out to be nothing, just an evening in my life, but what an evening!

I couldn't answer his request to "fuck me hard", I just looked at him and I guess in my eyes there must have been approval,

because he started to unbutton my pants and unzip to see my pussy.

Of course I was wearing panties, so I thought, "He's not going to take them off in public, is he? He publicly slid his fingers inside my pussy and at the same time took my hand to show me the bulge in his pants, which was shielded by his raincoat. I was completely fascinated, and we stroked each other for about five more minutes.

I get wet just writing about all this. It all seems so incredible and so long ago. Anyway, he always wanted more and more. He kissed and licked my eyes, my ears and my neck; all this in public so that everyone could see it. I never stopped him, I never did anything but join in. I stroked his penis, which was covered by his raincoat, and pulled it out, but there was no way to actually kiss him in public...

Suddenly he was buttoning us all up. He grabbed my arm and threw his other arm around me, right under my breasts. He whispered, "Okay, bitch, let's go. I'll fuck you like you've never been fucked before."

When the train stopped, we got off, and he walked or marched us to the end of the platform. Just past the end of the platform, there was a small tunnel with a little dim light on. It looked very shabby, but who cared. That was my seediest, sexiest fantasy come true. He marched me in there, I did what I was told, I was used to doing what I was told; my boyfriend at the time was very used to bondage!!. He kissed my lips, squeezing them, and then forced his long tongue to the back of my throat. After he pulled his tongue out, he smiled

naughtily and said, "Hey, baby, you do that with my tail, or you'll feel the end of my belt.

I said, "Yes, sir. I know, sir, I'm here to please you, sir."

"Turn and face the wall, bitch," he said, smiling, knowing I'll obey.

I turn around and feel him rip my panties off and take my shirt off. Then he takes my bra and leaves me naked on top. He slaps my breasts against the cold naked wall so that my nipples get hard when they come to life. Then he squeezes them so hard that I scream.

"Shut up, bitch," he says.

I bite my tongue, knowing that it will soon be of better use. He caresses my breasts again, and I'm wet, dripping wet, it's about to seep through my pants.

I didn't need to worry, although he grabbed the rest of my clothes and fingered my pussy. He whispers to me: "Well, my bitch likes it, and wants to be fucked as hard as possible. I'm mumbling, and he says, "Tell me you like all this, bitch."

I say, "Oh, sir, I love it all."

He says, "Tell me you want me to fuck you."

I say, "Sir, please fuck me, please, please fuck me, sir."

He spreads my legs and fists me from behind. My pussy opens up wide for him and it's so wet, I start to come over his fist. Meanwhile he sticks his penis up my ass, I scream, he

slaps my ass and pinches my clit and says: "Should I call the people who are standing 15 meters away?

I say, "Oh, no. "Please, sir, would you mind putting some cream on my ass? I'm a little girl."

He says, "Bitch, I ain't got nothing, but I'll use the juice from your pussy." Which he does, while dipping his penis again and again and again, so that I squirt at least twice. He spits, too, but it's hard right back. Then he turns me around and says, "Crouch down, legs bent, bitch."

I do as I'm told, now I'm shivering, not from cold, but from anticipation. I like it all. He opens my pussy wide and stretches it out so he can see right into it. Then he dips his tongue in it while fingering me at the same time.

And I'm like, "Please, sir, may I suck your penis?"

He laughs at me and says, "Ask me nicely, bitch, and ask me if you can have my cock next time, or you'll feel my belt.

Then I gently take his nine-inch bent dick in my hands. He's still fully clothed, while I'm completely naked except for my black stockings, garter belt and high heels covered in cum. Then I start to slowly and erotically massage, kiss and pinch his beautiful curved cock. Then I go down to his hard scrotum and lick his back while I stick two fingers up his ass and enjoy every minute of it.

Suddenly he grabs my hair and screams: "Stop playing the fool and suck my cock, you dirty little bitch".

I stop, shivering, and put all his nice bent cock in my mouth, sucking and sucking until it reaches my throat. He pulls at my hair and pushes my head down so that I almost gag on his amazingly hard curved cock. Slowly he lifts my head and I start erotically up and down again, pushing his cock in and out of my mouth. Never before had I tasted anything so delicious. He came fast and hard in my mouth and over my naked breasts. He grabbed my breasts and slapped them. Then he said "Bend over" and put his cock back in my ass and his fist in my pussy.

He came back in my ass again, then he took out a wet wipe, wiped himself off and left. I never saw him again.

WHATEVER YOU NEED

He knew what she needed even before she asked for it, but he did not want, needless to say, to see the pleading in her eyes as she struggled to form the words from her trembling lips.

He pulled her close, lifted her chin with a finger, looked directly into her watery blue and asked, "Tell me what you want, little one."

She hesitated for a moment and let his words sink into her soul: "I need a beating and a cuddle," she whispered.

He heard her words; he heard what she thought she needed, but he knew that she needed more. After the week she had had, she needed her head cleared of everything, everything but him.

He stroked her cheek with his finger and said with a forgiving smile, "We're not asking like that, are we?

A faint blush formed on her cheek as she smiled shyly and with a flutter of her eyelashes and asked in a low voice, "Sir, would you please spank me and then hold me for a while?

He noticed the gleam in her eyes where a lonely tear began to form. But he knew that she would not cry, not yet. He pulled her to his chest, kissed her on the top of her head and murmured into her hair: "I'll give you everything you need, my girl.

He held her for a moment before he lowered his mouth to her ear and whispered his instructions to her. She raised her head

to look up at him and nodded her lips softly and with a shy bite. Her unspoken submission, an unspoken "Yes, sir".

He made his way across the couch while waiting for her return. As soon as she entered the room, he sat upright and watched her with warm affection, and she knelt gracefully before him, holding the requested items in her open palms.

He began with the collar. He took the leather strap from her outstretched hand, reached behind her, gently brushed her hair away from her neck, and wrapped her in his possession. As the metal clasp snapped shut, a satisfied sigh escaped her lips unasked. He took the other two objects from their sacrificial palms and waved them to stand up. She rose and stood before him in dignified submission, waiting for his invitation to bend over his knee.

He noticed her anticipation, the redness in her cheeks increased, her chest rose and fell as she took a deep breath. He knew she was waiting, but he knew she needed this ritual, the ritual where there was no word in the world that counted except his own.

He patted his knee and waved for her to take her position. She went over a step to his side and then draped herself over his lap. With her body in the desired pose, he instructed her to cross her arms behind her back while he tied her hands with the leather cuffs he had requested earlier. Without her hands to support her, he could feel her sinking into him, and all her weight, even the invisible one she carried on her shoulders, fused into him. Her face was buried deep in the sofa cushion while she waited for the first blow.

She was almost surprised when the first blow came, and she gasped loudly. His hand kept pressing on her bottom, but apart from a muffled groan now and then, she hardly whimpered at all. He slapped her harder without letting up and filled her bottom with deep shades of crimson, but still, he felt her, she was still too present. He needed her to let go; she needed him to make her let go.

It was time for the paddle, the third item he had asked her for. All he had asked her for was a paddle; he had allowed her to choose the paddle she wanted. She had chosen the meanest and heaviest leather tool in his collection, and he smiled with secret pride. Normally, she would flinch at the mere thought of this weapon, but his girl knew what she needed, and he was more than willing to help her.

He gently stroked her burning bottom, the beating had been hard, but it hadn't been enough.

He lifted the paddle into the air and with one quick movement brought it hard on her reddened skin.

"Ouch!" she yelped.

Finally a reaction. She had to feel, let the pain swallow up everything else. He hit her again and again; every scream, every howl, every groan gave him an uncomfortable pleasure.

"Whatever you need, my girl."

And then, as if by magic, he could almost see the tension rolling off her body as she sank deeper into him, almost weightless, and from behind the pillow he could hear her

sobbing. He didn't let up; he let the paddle down on her harder and harder and felt her body tremble as the sobbing of the wrap went through her to his soul. She needed that. He needed her to let go, for her, for him.

He paddled, she moaned, he spanked, she cried, he beat, she let it all out, and the more he beat her, the lighter she became, until there was no sound, no weight, only her humble devotion to his kindly services.

He stopped, and she lay still on his body.

He scooped it up and entangled it in his arms. There was no sound other than her tattered, shallow breaths.

With one finger he wiped a lonely, stray tear from his eyes.

"Whatever you need, my girl."

IN THE DRIVING SEAT

I grabbed the steering wheel firmly with both hands. I had just passed my test last week and couldn't believe that he would allow me to drive his car, a brand new silver-grey Mercedes. This was my reward for passing my driving test and all his tests.

I didn't know where we were going. He gave the instructions, and I followed them. We had just entered a two-lane road, I shifted into fifth gear and felt the power of the car pulsating beneath me. The spinning engine together with its powerful look went straight into my pussy and I felt myself getting wet. I had to be careful though, I didn't want to damage his car and I didn't want to risk a penalty.

He was calm; apart from the instructions he had not said a word. Now that I was driving at 50 miles an hour, I didn't expect any conversation for a while. He reached over and gently pulled his fingers up my thigh, pushed up my skirt and felt my wet panties. I gasped as he gave me an appreciative smile and removed his fingers.

"Put your hands inside your panties and touch yourself," he ordered.

"But sir, I'm driving," I whispered halfway.

"Now", he said softly but firmly. I knew that tone of voice, it was his 'Don't make me tell you again' voice.

I held on to the steering wheel with one hand and slowly moved my hand down my waistband and into my now

soaked panties. I moved my fingers along my wet slit and teased my swollen clitoris. I moaned as I felt my breath accelerate.

"Eyes on the road," he commanded. I understood now. I had a tendency to close my eyes while masturbating. He wanted them to be open and to expand with excitement. I wanted to see him watching me.

After apparently 100 miles, but probably less than a mile, he ordered me to turn off at the next exit. He now let me drive with both hands and showed me the way to a quiet but not remote area. We parked in a large field near a B-road.

"Get out of the car", he ordered.

I obeyed and followed him as he led me to a nearby tree. Standing under it, he told me to lift up my skirt.

"Now masturbate for me." I took my hands in my pants, spread my swollen pussy lips and began to move my fingers across my smooth wetness. My cunt fluids poured down my thighs as I slowly inserted a finger into my inner sanctum. My clitoris throbbed as my thumb pressed down and I threw my head back with relish.

"Open your eyes," he reminded me.

"Now take off your panties and sit by the tree."

I sat down and knew how he wanted me. It was a position he had taught me the first day I met him. Knees bent, spread apart, flaunting my pussy for him.

"No, the other side," he pointed to the spot where he wanted me to sit.

My eyes opened wide. He wanted me to sit facing the traffic. My naked shaved pussy would be on display for every passing motorist. "Well", there was that voice again. I was moving around, legs spread, my pussy throbbing. He was in front of me, his position was no coincidence. He hid me a little from the public, but anyone who looked would know what I was doing.

"Look at me while you finger fuck yourself", his tone of voice commanding but gentle. I stared at him as I stuck two fingers inside my wet, aching cunt. I felt my juices flowing around my fingers as I rode them hard.

"I need to cum," I gasped.

"Not yet."

I kept fingering myself and teasing my clitoris with my other hand. I moaned loudly. I could have caused a 20 car pile-up and not even noticed.

"Please," I begged, almost sobbing.

"Don't stop," he almost growled at me.

I continued my attack on my tender, swollen cunt, my thighs were smooth from my distress. I gasped, my whole body trembled and I could feel myself cramping. I had to cum.

"Now you may stop", his voice deep and commanding.

He gave me his hand as he helped me get up. I trembled with desire, the need to let go.

"You come when I say," he whispered in my ear.

"Yes, sir."

He led me back to the car and opened the passenger door for me.

"I'm driving now," he smiled.

Oh, yes, he definitely was.

SUNDAY ON MY MIND

"You'll have to wait till Sunday, baby.

"Keep Sunday night free in your diary, Baby Girl.

These and numerous similar statements had made me itch for Sunday. But when Sunday finally arrived, nothing seemed unusual, and I began to worry that it was all just a big itch. As usual I got up first and did a short version of my daily stretching exercises, short because after breakfast we went to the gym together. After waking up all my muscles and joints, I went to the kitchen to bake some more of the croissants that I had baked from scratch as a weekend treat. While I set the table with yoghurt, fruit and blueberry jam, my thoughts wandered further and further into the time until this evening.

I called up the stairs to tell him breakfast was ready and began to throw together some leftovers to conjure up a light lunch for the road while I waited for him to come to me.

The croissants were a success, because seeing how much he liked them filled me with happiness and pride. Giving has always been my most important love language, so everyone I have ever been with has been showered with handmade gifts, cards, poems and homemade pancakes, cookies and other goodies. Only this time, with him, it was more than that. I had never given myself to anyone before, not in that way. Not so completely, so trustingly and so willingly. I loved being at his mercy, ready to fulfill every single one of his wishes and fantasies. We had discovered my natural submissiveness the summer before and since then we have been on a journey of discovery that has driven me further and further, until now

without reaching any hard limits. The development of our relationship and our excursions into perverse terrain changed me in ways I could never have imagined. I had no idea that I was carrying all this inside me. The soft toughness and the hard softness of being this slutty, submissive baby girl.

I knew that work was chaotic and that he was easily distracted in the best of times, but I really didn't think he could have forgotten his promises of today. Not that I even knew what those promises included. I was left in the dark, his power over me like a spiritual blindfold. Just the way I liked it. I always tried to get him to talk when he was mysterious, but actually I wanted to be surprised.

We went to the gym, spent a few hours getting tired and went home again. There was no mention of plans for tonight. I jumped in the shower and scrubbed myself with a sparkling shower gel anyway, one can only hope. After the shower I sat down with a book, but didn't really take in any of the words, I was far too distracted. I could now hear him rooting around upstairs. So maybe, after everything...

I was sitting with my back to the door when he finally came in. I pretended not to notice, but I felt a tingling all the way down my back. He put his hand on my shoulder.

"Come with me, baby girl, time for some fun

I slowly got up and went up the stairs. I noticed his presence behind me, his eyes on my back and my bottom. The flutter in my stomach almost made me giggle. I went into the bedroom. I noticed that the restraints under the mattress we had

recently invested in had been slightly adjusted, but nothing more than that. What had he been up to?

He had undressed.

His voice pulled me out of my thoughts, and his tone reminded me that I was in no position to ask questions. My role is to take orders. Speak only when spoken to. Never ask, always answer. My Lord. I'm a lump of clay that must be constantly shaped and reshaped by his hands. I am a piece in an interactive art installation, as well as a toy, like the massive purple dildo or the shiny nipple clamps. When I undressed, I could see him lifting the blindfold. He loosened the strap over my head, I felt the soft dark fabric replace my view of the room. This padded darkness filled me with a calm confidence. A feeling I had missed, a state I had longed for since he had mentioned Sunday.

"Give me your hands.

More padded restrictions on my freedom. He tightened the shackles on my wrists, but instead of taking me to bed as I had expected, he raised my arms above my head. I felt him fiddling with knots, and my arms were pulled forward and upwards.

Step forward.

He nudged me gently and I took a cautious step towards the force pulling on my hands. I felt my tits pressing against the cool white wood of the bedroom door. Somehow he had tied my hands to the top of the door, maybe even to the frame. I

sighed and felt my body settle down in the comfort of this lovingly inflicted discomfort.

Good girl.

And before I could even register what was about to happen, I felt a sharp slap on my bottom. The fire of impact made me gasp and I didn't even have time to close my mouth before the next slap. Even harder. The tip of the cut left a burning mark as he flicked it up just as it hit my soft skin. He paused. Gently he stroked my thighs with the tip of the crop, using the same tool that had just caused me such pain. He pulled the crop higher up my inner thigh until he patted my desperate pussy. I felt my whole body writhing to get more contact, more pressure out of that touch. He laughed knowingly. He would of course make me wait.

So... needy...', he said with feigned disapproval.

He pulled the crop away and brought it down hard again. I could imagine how red my bottom must be by now. At first the beating was slow, it increased in intensity but not in speed. He alternated between spanking and slowly massaging my sore cheeks. Then suddenly it rained down on me in a storm of sharper and duller slaps and blows. I was so stunned that I could not even move away from the impact. Not that that even brought it to a halt. Not that I even wanted him to stop, really. My twisted, pain-loving instincts made me lean into the path of the crop and enjoy every burning blow.

And then it was over as suddenly as it had begun.

A warm embrace from behind and his soft voice in my ear.

You did so well, Baby Girl, such a good girl. I'm so proud of you.

I gasp for breath and I can't completely free myself from my wonderful cocoon of searing pain.

Yeah? I managed to whisper.

You took it so well, and you looked so beautiful.

He was kneeling behind me, and I felt his hand between my legs.

I've never seen a pussy that wet before. It was literally dripping. Good girl. You enjoyed the beating, didn't you?

"Yes." was my slow exhaled answer. There was no point lying, my body had already betrayed me.

He reached up and my arms came down at the sides as I felt the rope slacken. He did not take the bonds of my wrists as he pushed me roughly onto the bed. He seemed to enjoy the first phase of his plan and that made me very happy. I had no idea how much more he had in store for me.

My arms were again above my head, each hand being pulled into a corner of the bed by the cuffs he had now attached to the handcuffs. A slight pull on my left foot, a set of cuffs was now also put around my ankles. I expected to be handcuffed at all four corners of the bed, as so often before. However, he grabbed my legs and pulled them up towards my chest. I had always been mobile by nature, but I silently thanked the gym teachers from my childhood for teaching me how to stretch. That was definitely not what they had in mind when they let

us practice the splits and told us again and again that it should hurt. I smiled at that thought. The pain is not that bad after all.

Once I was double bent, with ass and pussy in the air, he spread my legs and clamped each ankle to the corresponding wrist. Now that's what I call being exposed. When he started teasing me, I couldn't help but moan and whimper, so he quickly and deftly stuffed a gag in my mouth. It wasn't long before I felt the drool run down my chin.

The next half hour was a blurry picture of near-orgasms.

"Please, sir, can I come, sir?" Half words, half moans.

"No." would be the consistent response.

He held me nervously with a selection of vibrating toys, dancing fingers and finally the comfort of his warm, hard cock inside me. When I was told I could tip over the edge, I groaned through a deliciously intense and overwhelming release until I collapsed under him. It took a few minutes before I noticed how numb my legs were, still hanging at the wrists. He quickly untied me and we just stayed there, cuddling and smiling and kissing each other, a blissful grin lay on both our faces.

ROSE BUD

I wake up with your gentle breath on my neck, the feeling of your body pressed against mine and a soft grunt in my ear. Your hard cock is against me and my ass is instinctively lifted towards you, turning your body slightly so that I am lying on my stomach and you have access to me. My pussy is already dripping wet and ready for you to penetrate me. I don't need to say words because I feel your hand running down the length of my spine, sliding over my ass and pressing it before you give it a firm pat. Every fiber of my being is longing for you, goose bumps are rising on my skin, and a soft moaning escapes my lips as I feel your weight shifting. Your lips run over the skin of my shoulders, neck and upper back and pepper them with kisses. My body moves by itself and presses against you, my mind races; but I cannot speak. I feel your hardness against me and it is almost too much to bear. Your hand reaches down and encloses my throat, so that I have to turn my face to see you. So you can look into my eyes when the tip of your cock meets the entrance of my dripping wet pussy.

In my eyes you see my soul, carnal desire and passion. You push your cock up and down and tease me while I wiggle and try to get you inside me. A smile of lust goes over your face, a wicked grin, you can see everything, everything of me, exposed in front of you, wishing that you own me. You slide in, my face lights up with satisfaction and excitement. My whole body burns hot as you penetrate me, my breath stops in my throat until I let a groan escape. You are careful, methodical, restrained. You push yourself firmly against me, make my body cramp around your cock before you pull back

and slide in hard again. My body swings against you, intense waves of lust flow through me. I want more, I beg you with my eyes to fuck me with wild devotion, even though I know that you won't do that yet. You want to see the true side of me, the side I keep hidden, the submissive who lets you do everything with her and enjoys everything.

Her hand leaves my throat and a light sigh of disappointment leaves my throat. Your hard cock is still in me. You start to guide my body with your hands until my ass is high in the air, my back bent and my face in the pillows. Your hand again traces my spine and my body shakes while you stroke my ass. Your words break the silence of the morning like a wave breaking on the shore.

"Are you ready, my pet?" while your fingertips tap against my ass. I gasp and pant as I feel you spread my ass cheeks to see my virtually untouched hole. I let out a soft whimper and manage to nod yes.

Your voice booms as my body recovers and I say, "I need to hear it from you. I swallow a lump in my throat caused by fear, nerves and excitement.

"Yes, Daddy, I'm ready", I whimper as I feel cold drops of liquid hitting my asshole. I feel your finger starting to rub the lubricant on my ass, slowly and methodically. A shower of fear, anticipation and joy all in one, runs down my back and makes me shiver as I feel your finger pressing into my hole. I whimper as my body tense up.

" Shhh", your other hand rubs my back and caresses my bottom "You can do this for me, darling, relax I'll take care of

you." All of a sudden the tension in my body relaxes and my butt instinctively moves towards you and presses your finger You know that I'm ready, that I trust you. Your finger wastes no time pressing itself into my hole to open it for the first time and I moan. I almost forgot that your cock is still inside me, but this feeling makes me think of it and I push against you by bucking my hips into you as you start to finger my hole while I rock against your cock. It doesn't take long before you insert a second finger that continues to wind my hole and make it ready for your cock. You make it ready to take me, conquer me, take possession of every part of my body and willingly let it be given to you.

I feel an orgasm coming when you slip out of my pussy. A begging moan escapes my lips, and I feel your cock at the entrance of my asshole. Fear runs down my back again and my mind races because I think it will hurt that you are too big, my body tenses and prepares. You start pressing in your hands and spreading my ass cheeks.

"Easy, little girl, you can do it, you can take it." Your words calm my raging mind and I start to relax' while I shove the head of your cock up my ass. A mixture of pain and pleasure washes over me as I begin to come. You slowly push in my ass and try to bury your cock deep to fill me. Slowly my body gets used to the feeling and finds it more comfortable.

"That's your mine, take my dick, your tight little ass feels so good around my dick." When I hear you say this, my body shakes and trembles this time, there is no fear, only pleasure when I push myself back to you and force you all the way inside me, a scream and moans escape my lips, and then you

start to pump slowly at first, then to the point where you fuck my ass as hard and deep as you can. I moaned and begged you for more. I beg you to fill my ass with semen. You fuck my ass with wild abandon, slap and smack my ass cheeks, pull my hair and make me moan. My sperm drips down my legs until you come inside me, the pressure is intense and I scream with pleasure before we both collapse breathlessly on the bed.

DADDY'S LITTLE SLUT

I wake up too black, I get confused, disoriented. I feel the soft felt covering my eyes, I'm still blindfolded. I feel the leather cuffs around my wrists and ankles cuffing me, the spread eagle, to the four-poser bed. I test my cuffs pulling on them. They won't move. My jaw hurts from being broken by the ball gag you "silenced" me with. I hear footsteps, smell your perfume, I know it's you. I hear you giggling, your velvety voice echoing off the walls.

"Is Daddy's little cunt awake?"

I'm whimpering in affirmation, knowing the ball gag in my mouth will make me miss the words. My cunt aches and throbs in anticipation. They giggle again and I feel something cold slide up my slit and settle on my clitoris. I gasp in amazement at the cold, I know immediately that it is a bullet.

"What a dirty bitch you are, your pussy is already wet for me. For me it's always wet."

I hear you saying how you slap my titty and then pinch and twist one of my nipples, which makes me scream, because I know the pain only makes me more wet. I feel you kick away, and again I cry. Then it starts. I feel the folded leather of the crop going through my body. They rub my nipples lightly with it so that they start to move; then CIRCULATE! I whimper while you slap my tits. 10 I count in my head. 10 each. I feel your hands running over the reddened flesh, then I feel cold metal on my skin and try to pull me away; in vain you have tied me up. I feel you grab my right nipple first, without mercy, I feel you pinch it to make sure it is good and

hard. Next, I feel a sharp pain as you apply the clamp. I whimper and then I feel you slapping my pussy hard, it stings.

"Thank my cunt, thank Daddy for the clamps, you dirty, wet, fucking little whore." I moan and I manage to whimper,

"Thanks, Daddy," my words muffled by the ball gag.

I feel a second clamp mincing and again I groan my thanks through the ball gag. The chain connecting the two clamps is so short that it pulls my titties together and pulls my nipples only 2 ½ or 3 inches apart, and every move makes my big D-sized titties bounce and wobble, pulling the clamps hard on my nipples.

I hear a soft click when you turn the bullet to the lowest speed. I pant and wiggle while the slow vibrations of the egg tickle my clitoris. A soft moaning escapes my lips, my titties giggle and pull on my nipples, the sharp pain only increases my arousal. I groan through the gag again,

"Thanks, Daddy."

I can feel that you shocked my face with that crop. You're stroking it along the length of my body, then you flick each breast so that they rattle the chain and pull on my erect nipples. I feel the crop run up my next right leg and then snap at my inner thigh, I try to scream, but the ball gagged me. My back arches a little and the egg presses harder against my clitoris. I feel the crop, at the speed it is running, landing another blow on the inside of the thigh of my left leg. I moan, I

cry through my gag and beg you to stop; this gives me 6 strokes of the crop 3 on each leg.

I feel the egg vibrating faster now, my body is bulging and I moan. I want to be fucked, I would like to have your rock hard throbbing cock inside me and I want to cum over your big thick cock. I want it so bad that I start begging, I hear you giggling and I get 12 more strokes. The first 6 land on my chest, the others on my inner thighs. I beg you

"Please Daddy, please fuck me. I'll do anything for your cock! Please!" the gag dampens my "please!"

I scream while you turn the egg up to the highest setting. I moan and wiggle, my tits stick out, my back arched, my pussy completely exposed.

"Please, I'll be right there! Please fuck me, I'll do anything!"

You put the egg down, and my body falls like lead. You whisper in my ear,

"What a little bitch you are... ...something for my dick?"

I whimper and nod and wonder why I promised something... I feel you lifting my head and removing the ball gag.

"I'll tell you which cunt, do you want my dick? Then you have to suck it and swallow all my sperm. Then I'm gonna fuck you, but there's a catch."

I whimper

"Would you like to meet the catching bitch?"

I hold my peace for one second too long and the harvest falls on my pussy.

"Do you want to be a whore?"

"Yes, yes please Daddy, please tell me what I have to do to deserve your beautiful cock!"

"While you suck my dick, this is what happens."

You knock the egg with the goiter that pushes it up against my clit.

"and you mustn't cum, if you cum I won't fuck you."

You take a deep breath and I whimper.

"After I fuck you and make you cum around my dick, I'm going to put this big 10-inch vibrator on your harness and ram it into your pussy, and you'll wear it all night long without coming. In the morning I'm gonna turn it up high while I fuck your tight little virgin ass. You still want to cum tonight, cunt?"

I'm whimpering and nodding for you to spank me again,

"Answer me bitch"

"Yes, Daddy, I still want to cum."

"Good. Now open your mouth and suck."

You say you're gonna stick your dick down my throat and start fucking my face.

BRAT

She was standing in the corner, her bright red butt turned towards him. He knew from the way she breathed that she was trying to control her carnal nature. He also knew that her ass was burning down to her pussy and that if he stood up now and grabbed her between her legs, she would open wide for him and his fingers would be covered with her juices.

He didn't mean to make her ass so red, but, man... she could drive anybody crazy who was acting all bratty sometimes. She just got too high and mighty for her own good and needed to be taken down a few notches. He was just the one who was supposed to do it. The only problem was that he was now as horny as she was, but she should be punished for talking back and being a pain in the ass!

He sat there and watched as she took a deep breath and tried to gather her mind around him, stroking his cock the whole time. Finally she seemed to calm down and he called her to him. She hesitantly walked towards him, and when she sat down in front of his chair, she knelt down before him. "Suck my dick, bitch" were the only words that came out of his mouth, she took it in her mouth immediately.

She took it deep until his cock hit the back of her throat and her face was buried in his groin. Then she took her tongue and pressed it against his vein as her mouth began to work on his shaft. He leaned back and just let her do her work, this time he enjoyed it and didn't help. She sucked and licked his cock and moved her mouth down and took his balls in her mouth and sucked them in before she took his cock back in her throat. She

sucked him until he started to come, then she pulled his cock out and made his cum run all over her face, covering herself with his white hot cum. She took her fingers to her face and wiped some off her cheek, brought her fingers to her mouth, sucked them in and licked his cum off them.

She had to cum so badly now... he knew it, too. Between the ass-whipping that still burned her ass and pussy and sucked it off, she felt like she would burst with sperm if she wasn't released soon. He told her to go back to her corner...his sperm dried on her face...she started to say something and then thought better of it. She sulked and did as she was told. He got up and got a few things... then he walked over behind her He reached between her legs and felt her pussy, his hands felt her juices on her thighs as she ran out of her pussy. Her pussy was dripping with pussy juice, she moaned and opened herself to him at his first touch.

She felt something go up inside her pussy... and then leaving her. Suddenly, she felt it go up her ass. She almost came right away, but he bent over and whispered in her ear that she wasn't allowed to cum yet. The intense pain and joy she felt when her ass was taken that way was almost too much. But she tried so hard to be a good girl for him. He told her to keep the plug in her ass until he took it out.

He started spanking her again... not as hard as the first time, this time just to reawaken the nerve endings. The whole time he was spanking her again, she was begging him to please let her cum. He never answered her... he just kept telling her that she was his bitch, his whore... if he wanted to play with her

pussy and ass for ten hours... without her coming... that's what he would do.

He'd turn her around, grab her nipples, take her to the coffee table, twist and pinch her as they walked... ...she failed miserably at not screaming. Every time she screamed out loud, he just turned more and more. He put her on the table, right where his hand would get a good pat on her pussy and clit. He started to spank her... he managed again and again not to slap her clitoris, which she wanted so much. His fingers snapped her plug that was up her ass so that she moaned and asked him to please cum... He slapped and rubbed her pussy lips until he finally hit her clit. He barely put his finger over it when she begged again... this time with tears in his eyes... she needed to cum so badly...

He reached down, pinched her clitoris hard...told her: "Come now, my bitch...come for me. The orgasm after the orgasm wore down her body as he slipped into her and felt her claw on his cock and squirted repeatedly so that she became senseless afterwards. He helped her into bed, and as they lay together, she promised him that she would behave much better from now on. maybe.

A NIGHT WITH A SEXY BARTENDER

Angela is my favorite, although I like her all of them. To say she's petite is an understatement.

She could pass for a teenager. Well, for me, anyway, it's not what attracts me about her, it's the tattoos and the hair and the very pretty face. She's a bit feisty, which she can't stand the boss, but it works for me.

I am retired. Old enough to be her grandfather, but every day when she comes to work, she comes right up to me and hugs me. And I like that. I like it a lot. Every day during the farewell hug I whisper to her: "Come by my place when you get off work. She laughs, pushes me away and just blows it off. It's all a big joke. But the regulars are very protective of the girls.

So, Angela's boyfriend works in the oil fields somewhere and is away for three weeks and then home for a week. We can always say that when he is at home, she comes to work with a smile and a more relaxed attitude. She and I are friends through social media and occasionally send each other PMs. Nothing that her boyfriend shouldn't see. Very innocent stuff.

Well, last week, when the boyfriend was gone for about ten days, I got a short video of her. It was a slow striptease. The shirt was the first one. She pulled it over her head and then shook her long brown hair to make it straight. Next came the shorts. I had seen her wear them several times at the bar. Tight blue denim shorts that really showed off her cute little bottom.

The bra strap and the thong. She took her time. I was glued to my phone. Her tits were perfect A-cups with cute nipples. On the video, she crawls close to the camera and starts rubbing her clit.

"You like that?" she asks. "I like that," she says.

She turns her back to the camera and shows this cute little butt. No tan lines.

Okay, I was as tough as I could at the time, but I wondered why she sent me this. My ego made me believe that she was really into me. My common sense asks why? And why? Why would she send this to me? There was nothing in our history to suggest such a thing.

Back on the tape she danced, looked into the camera and said, "I can't wait for you to come home, baby. I really can't wait." She licked her fingers before she squeezed them up her pussy.

Back home? Baby? That answered all my questions. That video was for her boyfriend.

Now I felt stupid. This old guy who thinks a young woman might be attracted to him I watched it to the end and then turned it off. I debated whether I should watch it again, but decided that it really wasn't the right thing to do. I went to bed feeling old and ashamed.

Around midnight I got a lunch break. It was Angela.

"OMG!!!! Excuse me. I'm so embarrassed. Please forgive me."

"There's nothing to forgive."

"Apparently, it was for Taylor."

"He's a lucky guy.

"I'm so sorry.

"When I saw it wasn't for me, I stopped looking at it. I've already deleted it." I lied.

A long time till the next message.

"Did you think it was for you? "I mean, did you think it was for you? ...why..."

"Skip it, okay? My mistake."

"Look, I'm sorry."

"I'll see you tomorrow." And I hung up the phone and tried to sleep.

I figured it was better than going to the bar the next day. I didn't want to embarrass her or me. Marvin called me around 4:30.

"Are you coming into the office?"

"Nah... I got a few things to do here today."

"Dude, you retired! Projects can wait till tomorrow." Marvin's forty and has a hot roommate and is responsible for maintaining a large government agency.

"I just can't make it, Buddy."

"I love you, buddy. If you need anything, let me know."

I didn't go in the next day either. At 6:00, I got a text from Angela. "Where are you?"

"Out playing golf," I lied.

"Okay. I just thought you were avoiding me."

"Well... maybe a little."

"Why?

"Can't really explain. I feel stupid, because I thought you sent it to me on purpose. Silly old man."

"I'm sorry."

"No problem."

"You're not playing golf, are you?"

"I've got to go."

There's no fool like an old fool.

The phone rings at midnight. "Hello?"

"Open your front door."

"I can't get past here. I'd never hurt you," she said as she invited herself in. She put down her bag and gave me my usual hug, but it was much longer than usual. She looked at me through the tears in her eyes. I wiped them away. I had seen that look before, by chance from another Angela. I bent

down and kissed her lips. Beautiful, soft lips. She opened her mouth and I felt her tongue sting as she went in and out.

I led her by the hand down the hall into my bedroom. She stood before me in the light of the little lamp by my bed. I took off her clothes. These breasts... these magnificent A cup breasts... I left her panties on.

Once on the bed, I tied her hands behind her head and fastened them to the hook that was there for that reason

"Wait a minute..."

"Shhh...trust me."

I started with the Warteburg wheel. I circled her barely-existing tits several times before I got to the nipples. The fidgeting began. The wheel always gets her. Down her belly, around her navel, to the panty line. I followed the wheel over her body and followed the elastic waistband of her transparent panties.

Her breath became deeper. Long breaths.

I began to gently rub her clitoris through her panties. Sometimes I barely touched her. Her hips began to move seemingly involuntarily when I touched her. Within minutes she was close to it, so I stopped. I felt her slip away. But her disappointment didn't last long when I started again. Within seconds, she was on the verge of coming. This time I let her down. She was hunched over. I was glad she was tied up.

When her breathing returned to normal, I went to the foot of the bed, stuck my thumbs in the waistband of her panties and

began to take them off. She raised her hips and allowed me to remove them with one movement. My index finger found its way into her pussy, where it started the same technique at her G-spot. Again it didn't take long. I took my magic wand, turned it on low and placed it on her clitoris while I licked, ate and fingered her pussy. The sensation was too great and she exploded on my bed. Small drops of female sperm squirted out of her orifice.

When she was in the middle of her second orgasm, I rammed my cock into her and fucked her as best I could. As I was moving towards a climax, so was she. I shot my load and she had orgasm number three. Maybe not as intense as number two, but enough to make her squirt a little more. I rolled off her and left a trail of cum on her leg. When I recovered, I licked up our juices and then let go of her wrists. She was exhausted and lay motionless for a few minutes before getting up and getting dressed.

"When we got to the front door, she turned around and said, almost laughing, 'I've never been so fooled. I've never been fucked like that before."

"Good."

"It can never happen again."

"I know."

We kissed and I pinched her right nipple. She went to her car and drove away.

TEN STEPS

The phone rang once, and I pressed "end" on my cell phone. That was the signal to get ready. I'd just been out for 10 minutes. And it would take her 10 minutes to get ready: Strap her ankles to the table legs, put the blindfold on, slip her wrists into the rope loops and pull her up to tie her down.

But even before that she had to lay out the champagne, a glass and an ice bucket. The chair had to be positioned with the right wrist cuff and tied to the removed table leg. The toys had to be organized, including the special toy that I would find when I arrived. The towels had to be put aside when needed.

As I stopped in front of the old Victorian house, I went over the instructions again and made sure I was prepared for the slightest infraction. I rang the bell again - just one ring - and hung up. It was the last signal indicating my entry into the house.

Step one: door open. One for 10.

The apartment was tastefully furnished, as befits the home of a designer. A gentle clash of 19th century bourgeois grandeur and 20th century modernist minimalism. Light flowed through the lace curtains and poured down on a quietly waiting figure in the middle of the dining room.

She was soft, curvaceous and dressed in a black cocktail dress, pale skin set off by golden hair with a refined tuft. Her black stockings began just below the hem, revealing a flash of soft flesh cut by six suspenders. They disappeared in black leather pumps with a thin, one-centimeter high heel. Their arms were

stretched out over a table with falling leaves in handcrafted style, deeply radiant and warm with years of wear. Nylon cords were attached to her back legs and wrapped around her wrists. Her ankles were tied to the nearby table legs with black velcro straps. Around her eyes was a colourful silk scarf in a complex botanical William Morris print. Deep shades of red and green and earthy browns were entwined.

Steps two and three: ready and in position. Three for 10.

I sat down in the chair, positioned as I asked her, to her right hand. The wine was chilled and ready to drink, and with a gentle "POP" the pressure that had built up over years of storage in deep, dark rooms was released in a hurry. It frothed gently as I filled the lonely crystal flute that stood beside the bucket.

Fourth step: Wine. Almost half of the requirements were met with full marks.

After I emptied a second flute, I stood up and walked around her lying body. I did not yet dare to touch her, but checked my possibilities. Her luscious lips were accessible at the right height. Her delicious ass was also lying and a little on my father's side I imagined her naked pussy swollen in anticipation. It was time to check out the surprise request.

With a gentle stroke over her round ass I lifted the fabric to reveal a light blue gemstone that had nested in her wrinkled asshole.

Fifth step: jewel-studded butt plug in place. Halfway home.

With that light contact, she squirmed a little, and she sighed with a heavy sigh. But this was not the right moment. I was still thinking about what to do next when I saw the ring gag.

I gently opened her mouth with my fingers, put the leather strap under her head and put the big rubber ring between her lips. Her tongue danced right in her teeth, which she dutifully opened wide to accommodate the apparatus.

I opened and took off my suit jacket, unbuckled my belt and unzipped my fly. The noise took her breath away. And as I pulled my cock out of my boxers, she made a sound like swallowing, preparing, anticipating...

I slipped into the ring myself and got hard as the wetness and warmth of her open mouth enveloped me. Caressing gently at first, then faster, I bucked with my hips against the table and into her mouth, stretching my hips against the table and into her mouth, reaching down to calm me with the back of her head, wrapping my fingers around her thick locks of hair and forming a ponytail grip to control her pace and flinch when it got too intense. Several minutes of sheer joy.

When she retired from the table, some saliva came out of the corner of her mouth and gathered on the table. I pushed the linen napkin that had been under my glass in front of her mouth to soak up everything that came out of her mouth. It was a really nice table after all.

Step six: Suck me. Done.

As I walked behind her, I pushed her legs apart and rubbed myself up and down the naked thigh area between her

stockings and the silk underwear gusset. She got tired and stood under a jackknife in this position for almost 30 minutes. But now my time had come. "She'll have all day to rest when I'm finished with..." My thought ended when I saw the wet spot on her underwear. She was growing fast, and little trickles of girls were peeking out and starting to descend her thighs. To help the process, I rubbed my thumb firmly in place and felt more wetness penetrate the silk. Underneath, her lips spread to reveal more of the moisture that was collecting inside her, and the trickles turned into full streams of semen. I now pressed harder and faster on her clitoris and jerked her through the silk of her soaked panties while listening as her breathing was replaced by a hoarse scream that was replaced by an open throat scream. As her climax began to break on her, I stopped and stepped back as she twisted against the shackles.

Seventh step: her first edge.

With this I folded up her skirt and pulled down her soaking wet panties to reveal her thick wet pussy lips. A thick string of coagulated girl cum hung heavily between them and I leaned in for a taste. I slid my tongue around the entrance to her pussy and licked up spoons of her abundant wetness, which now covered my clean-shaven face. When I saw an opportunity to move on to step nine, I pulled back the jeweled butt plug and replaced it with my tongue as I massaged her perineum, looking for a clue to her orgasm that she was not allowed to reach.

It didn't take long: between the pressure of my tongue in her ass and my thumb right underneath it, she began a harrowing

release that made her work even harder and bulged even more. Even more shaking. More sperm. More labored breathing. Still no orgasm.

Eighth step: her second edge. Now it was mine.

I swallowed another glass of wine. Her whole step was open and wet, her ass slightly open and ready and I had to make one last decision. I looked at the toy, chose a string of purple beads, oiled them and carefully stuck them one by one into her delicious ass until only the pull ring was visible. Time to fuck.

My cock was still hanging half-hard outside my pants, but with a few short moments of reinsertion through the ring gag I was prepared. Pressing my cock head between her lips, it took a light push to get into the moisture of her pussy, which was warmer and wetter than her mouth. She let go another breath as I went deep inside her and felt her ass cheeks against my pelvis, pressing my balls against her clitoris. Then again, and again, and again, and again, and again, and again, faster and faster and faster until the sound of the meat tapping echoed from the high ceiling above the dining table, shaking and creaking with every beat.

The first hints of my climax began deep in my groin, with growing pressure from the root of my penis. When I felt this first swelling, I tugged on the beads until the first ones came out of their squeezed assholes. A squeak, followed by rhythmic moaning. My second cramp made me twitch inside her, but she was distracted by the second bullet pulled out of her asshole. At the third and fourth cramp, a dribble from my

front jaw mixed with her already considerable wetness, which intensified as I pulled the next balls out of her ass.

Seeing her wrinkled asshole open up and give up the smooth purple plastic was a stunning contrast to my cock crawling in and out of her pussy.

With the fifth, sixth and seventh cramp, I tried to resist the original urge to fill them with my sperm and instead concentrated on tugging on the next bead - but not removing the next bead until I knew I was under control. As I pushed silently and the crisis built up, I leaned into it and accelerated as fast as I could as if my life was at stake. Any pretense of tickle was gone now that I was fucking her as hard and as fast as I could. With the eighth and ninth cramp, I knew that she was as close to me since my arrival as she had been since I arrived. I reached under her until the point where her legs parted, and jingled my fingers across her clitoris as fast as I could in a feverish rhythm that escalated her screams to screams.

Then I stopped. I pressed firmly against her, but remained calm for several minutes.

Finally I pulled away from her and walked around the side of the table. I looked into her pale blue eyes, grabbed the champagne flute and began to stroke my cock. My eyes looked deep into hers, I increased the pressure and speed of my stroking until the ultimate throb came over me. With my left hand I reached for her hair again so she couldn't look away while I shot thick and hot into the glass, my sperm mixed salty with the sweet champagne. She watched as I took

a breath and placed the glass next to her head on the linen napkin.

Step nine.

She was still hyperventilating, so I filled the glass with the rest of the champagne and tipped the empty bottle into the ice bucket. She could drink it after I left.

Without saying a word, I pulled up my own trousers, tucked and arranged everything and closed the zipper. The light grew dim, so I turned on a lamp. As I walked towards her, I saw her back lift, her legs wiggle and sweat flow over her own face. She had been finger and tongue fucked, her ass had been probed, and she was forced to suck me off. I didn't come inside her. I didn't force her to come. In fact, she had hardly moved. I hadn't said a word to her. And I left her panting and tense at the table because I knew I was done with her for the day.

I took a rigging knife from my pocket and cut the rope on her right hand, then folded the knife back together, grabbed my coat and went out to the car. When I got in and turned the ignition, I pressed the redial button, let it ring once and hung up.

Step 10. Sleep well.

MARKED

I know you're here with someone else. I know we just met for a friendly drink, which was a painful exercise in self-control. I also know that you're standing in the corner taking a breather from incessant small talk.

I get up from the bar with a glass of wine for you, the same label you had in the restaurant when we met. It's not a great party - rather stuffy, to be honest, so I'm determined to have some fun just for us.

You are wearing this dress: short, black, a little sparkling, a little glittering, dipping to reveal a worthy measure of cleavage. Your thick, reddish-brown hair is made simple. You are possessed by a quiet elegance that drives me crazy. You turn around and smile as I approach, and I hand you the glass.

"Thank you", you say shyly and look down while I look at you. "Kind of a boring party, huh?" I ask. You nod. People huddle around your date, his attraction draws attention with little effort. "You've got a great guy there," I say and smile. You smile back softly.

I put my hand around your arm and whisper, "Would you like some air?" It's not a question. We walk slowly to the veranda overlooking Newport's Cliff Walk. The surf beats in the night, and a cool breeze comes in from the ocean. It's enough to cool you down, so I take off my suit jacket and drape it over your shoulders.

While I do this, I close the front firmly and pull your body sharply against me and press my lips against yours. Your eyes will be wide open in surprise, then sit down in an expression of satisfaction as my tongue snakes into your mouth. I lead my left hand into your hair and slide my right hand down the front of your beautiful body.

They seem to be protesting, but I whisper again: "Shhhhhhhhh... relax", and kiss you deeply again.

My right hand follows your figure to below the hem of your dress and along your thighs, then back up again, grabbing the hem of your dress and lifting it over your hips. Instinct stretches your legs against my hand and you pull back slightly, but only slightly. I let my fingertips slide under the string of your thong and look deep into your eyes to soothe you.

Then a long pause as I press my lips against your lips and pull your head closer to mine, my fingers tremble in anticipation of slipping behind the triangle of fabric that covers your delicious prize.

My hand slides effortlessly down your smooth hill. The silky fabric slides along the back of my hand. You are warm, and as my fingers slide down deeper, I feel the temperature of your skin rise as the blood rushes to your pussy. In four centimetres it is warm to hot.

Then a crack. It's wet. Then it's wet. And hard. Tiny lips outline you, open and intentional. Your skin tingling with the new sensation of my fingers against your swollen clitoris. I slip inside you and the wetness thickens.

To avoid drawing too much attention to us, I press my lips back over your open mouth, from which moans and choked screams emanate. The sounds continue, but I swallow them down as the sky swallows smoke.

Now your hips press against my hand, which crunches deeply to force my fingers into the thick pool of desire you carry within you. My fingers break a seal and your sperm slides along my hand and out of your body, hot and thick and delicious, then in a thin stream down your thigh.

"Now be a good girl and come for me."

With these few words, your body replies. Your muscles contract and force the thick cream into the palm of my hand. I smell your sex. For now you are mine, and the world is unimportant. You dance on my hand and sway at the pulse of my fingertips.

"One more time."

Words grab you, and again you wiggle in my hand and let go, your voice is tense, your nipples harden and rub raw against the silk of your dress. You bend your knee against the hardness in my trousers, but I push your leg down again. You must not touch it.

"Again." I hiss for the third time - a little scary and hard - and you break.

Your head trembles and your body convulses. The wetness is pouring out of you and soaking through the French cuff of my shirt. The air is thick with you.

You have drawn me.

As the third wave passes, I grab you firmly in my arm to hold you up. You lean into a deep kiss, but I push my smooth fingers into your mouth, then I press them deeper with my lips. "Taste your pleasure", I croak and lick the cream from my hand. It is mixed with your saliva and drips onto my other cuff.

You pull my hand out of your mouth and jump forward to keep your fingers in, but I pull it back far enough that you can turn your eyes towards me. You want more. So I grab your hand and put it under your skirt, load your fingers with your cream, hesitate for a moment and use it to circle your open pussy to get even more wet. You pant, then press your pussy against your fingers to collect even more.

With a jerk I pull your hand up against your wrist and hold it between us. In this moment I see you and smell and taste you. I have you all to myself. And with a heavy look in your eyelids, you agree with me.

Our tongues meet and lick your fingers clean before our lips press together and share the last drops of you.

Then we breathe. The ocean breathes on us, cools us down and brings us back. On the porch. To the big old house. To the people. To the small talk. To the realization that I am marked.

And that nobody knows it but you.

Without disturbing the sheet that covers your body, I slide my hand down your warm form. Your curves intoxicate me. The scent of your sweat fills my senses: sweet with a subtle undertone. Animal desire. And before my fingers pass your hips, I smell your sex. Clean, salty and drug-like in its effect. Blood flows from my brain and floods my cock. Unconscious desire clouds my senses and I pull back the sheet and reveal your masterpiece of a body glowing alabaster in the moonlight.

But you are not made of stone; you are also flesh and blood and desire and need. My need is to drink your sperm. To bathe my face and beard in the sweet liquor that your desire distils. To hear this crescendo of voice and screaming and moaning and crying, blended into a harmonious, raw symphony of liberation and renewed desire. The music continues until we both say it stops.

Her legs are firmly closed; such a shy, good girl. And with some effort I open your thighs to reveal the object of my hunger. You are swollen and red from the blood that has also left your brain. A whiff of creamy liquid drips from the underside of your pussy down your perineum to your other secret place. And I tilt my head to kiss your kitten deep Just like I kissed your mouth, but with a gentler pressure at your entrance. I open you with my lips. Taste you with my tongue.

Fuck you with my tongue.

Your hands grasp my head and pull me into you. Your hips sway to force my cock-like tongue deeper and deeper. Your climax flows like the rushing rapids of a mountain river, and I

lick your cream with a mighty thirst. The skin of your lips is irritated by my scratchy beard. You feel the tingling burning as I cleanse more and more girls from your thighs.

"Fuck me, Daddy," you say breathlessly. The bed is now drenched in sweat and desire. "Watch me, sweet girl," I say softly. Slowly I stand before you, my clothes drenched in sweat, your wetness and my own excitement. First comes the suit jacket. Then, after I lower my suspenders, the French cuffed shirt. I stretch out my hand so you can undo the cuff links. "Slower, baby," I purr. You smile, and your graceful fingers carefully release the small figures from my cuffs - the devil on my left hand, an angel on my right - and place them on the bedside table. You kneel down on the bed to unbutton my shirt, and while your back is straightened, I lift up your soaked nightgown and reveal your irresistible body. The skin is soft, the breasts with the large wrinkled nipples glow perfectly in the light, the curves envelop your hips and your exquisite bottom and hide your most secret place.

You unbuckle my pants, which fall to a puddle on the floor, and you enclose the outside of my tight boxer shorts to feel the agonizing state of my cock. Your touch burns and soothes, angry and calming. Finally we are here together, and yet we have lost ourselves to desire. Your hands trace the muscles of my legs to free the socks from my calves. You breathe in quickly as you feel my calves bending and tightening, and you bend forward to put your lips on the swelling between my thighs.

"Daddy, please," you coo, and I can't resist your upward glance. "Yes, sweet girl. Please suck me." And with long,

graceful fingers you free my cock from the saturated tissues - a mixture of abundant sweat and a river of precedent - and push it into your mouth. I faint. Your mouth is heavenly: you suck, lick, and breastfeed with puckered lips to suck the precum out of me, salty and clean and slippery. From the corners of your mouth, excess sweat comes out and gives a silvery shimmer to the beads of sweat that collect on your face. Any more of this and I will flood your mouth with more than just precum.

"Sweet girl, it's time," I say, lifting your face gently up by your chin to meet my eyes. "Oh Daddy, I want to, but I'm afraid," you beg, a slight wiggle in your voice. "I will take care of you, sweet girl. Do not be afraid." And you smile and nod for me, really the best, sweetest girl from the mountains that this town-born daddy could wish for.

In the moonlight, you slowly turn your body around and present me the magnificent globes of your ass. I am speechless at the sight of the perfect curves and the sensual cleft that gently tapers down to meet the creamy entrance of your kitten. I have dreamed of this moment. I have dreamed of this moment. I have tried to prepare for this moment, but I am still overwhelmed with longing and appreciation. We're finally here. And finally I can help you to feel what you have wished for so long, but entrusted only to me.

"Spread your bottom, baby," I say. And with these supple fingers, you gently pull your butt apart to reveal a tiny wrinkle. I see the streams of Girlcum on your legs, similar to the stream of Precum dripping from my dick. And your

bottom is covered with a thick glaze of Girlcum waiting to be tasted.

Hungrily I press my face between your cheeks and press my lap onto the tiny knot. You moan. As I get bolder, I press the tip of my tongue into your pulsating tightness until I feel the muscles dividing. I'm very light in your butt. Your voice becomes higher and a choked cry of lust escapes from your throat. Without removing my tongue, I slide two fingers into your tight pussy and massage the soft tissue inside. My tongue senses the massive orgasm that collects deep inside you: Your brain, nerves, flesh, heart, blood signal reaches its peak and sets the tiny ring of muscles that flutters and pulsates around my tongue.

"Oh fuck, Daddy, here I come! I purr! I'm purring!"

This is the moment. In an instant I stand up and position the head of my precum-soaked cock at the entrance to your ass. Another wave of the climax drives your face into bed and opens your ass just a little more. You are ready. And with gentle pressure I push into you.

The velvety smoothness of your ass is bliss. All the moments that led to this one are repeated in my closed eyelids. Eyelids closed because seeing would diminish the feeling. And nothing has a right to feel this good. Nothing has ever felt so good. Their rippling wave from climax to climax has never sounded so good.

Your ass is milking the sperm out of my dick. And I can't stop myself.

You feel the heat building up inside you before I can catch my breath to make a sound. Then I suck in oxygen and I'm like, "Oh fuck, baby! Oh fuck, oh fuck, oh fuck!" I scream. The windows are open and no doubt the whole neighborhood can hear us. "FUCK, BABY, FUCK, I CAN'T STOP!" And you crown a final wave of climax that makes the last drops of semen pulsate

We are both drenched in sweat and stink of sex. The smell hangs like magnolias blooming in the humid summer air of Carolina. I'm wobbly on my feet as the endorphins crawl and fade. My brain collapses in a fraction of a second before my body collapses behind yours, my cock stuck in the crevice of your soaked and slippery ass. Finally, we've marked each other.

In the calm air and moonlight we lay panting and slippery. Entwined in wafer-thin cotton. I stroked over your lush curves, with my back to the door and your head resting on my right arm. The fever of desire is broken.

For the moment.

CUMSLUT DIARIES

I sent an e-mail to one of my respondents. It was a fairly old e-mail, and I wasn't sure if someone was on the other end of my inquiry. To my surprise, I received a reply to my e-mail. I sent a simple email, pointing out that I was still looking for a cock and that I was an insatiable bitch who was willing to submit completely to another man who would be dominant and use me like the bitch I am.

The answer I received was from a frequent visitor to Savannah (actually Tybee Island, a beach community just outside Savannah). He said that he and his friends often come to Tybee for the weekend and they are interested in using a submissive bitch for a few days.

They gave me a time and a place, and I have to admit my heart was in my throat when I knocked on their front door. They made me feel comfortable, gave me a rum drink in their bar and made small talk for a few minutes. Then the fun started.

One of them came up behind me and told me to take my clothes off. When I turned around, two naked men stood behind me, their hard cocks dangling and swaying like erotic metronomes. I could not get out of my clothes fast enough. They pressed me on their knees and rubbed their cocks in my face. I only got a fleeting taste of cock because they were more interested in teasing me than fucking my mouth. There were four of them, but only two were playing with me while the other two were sitting on the sofa, laughing and drinking rum. Someone clicked a pair of leather cuffs on my wrists and

fastened them behind me. I was on my knees, crazy horny to suck, but they were teasing my mouth with their hard cocks. Finally I got my mouth on one of the huge cocks that were torturing me and started sucking and moaning. I want them to know what a slut I was. I was looking forward to an evening of wanton sexual abandonment. I wouldn't be disappointed.

They lifted me onto a large coffee table, about 5' X 5' in size, with the top of the table only about a foot off the floor. I was kneeling behind me with my hands secured as they placed an ottoman with me on the table and pushed me over the belly first onto the ottoman, still kneeling with my hands behind me. My face was accessible from one side of the coffee table and my bottom hung down from the other side. I could see that they had done this before. I had sucked my cock a bit, but I had never had anal sex before. I did not know what to expect. They put a barstool in front of me and used my mouth for a few hours while sitting on the barstool, feet on the coffee table. They fucked my mouth and called me their dirty whore. Sometimes when they came they would reach for a fist full of hair and bury their tails in my throat while pumping their charges into my mouth and throat. I had a really good time, I was so horny. I just got hornier as the night went on.

They had all fucked me in the mouth several times and they were getting rowdier by the minute. Then they started talking about fucking me. I begged them to just fuck me in the mouth, but they had invented their rum-soaked brains. I wanted to be fucked in the ass. One of them stuck his dick in my mouth so I could make it stiff again, and another one started fucking me in the ass with his fingers. It wasn't too long before I started riding on his finger like he was a cock. That was around the

time that the fat cock in my mouth switched to my ass. I was ready, he slipped in with a little effort. At first it hurt a little bit, I couldn't tell how much was inside me, but it felt like I was full and he was down. At first I moaned slowly like a whore until he hit me so hard that I grunted with every stroke. Another cock stuck in my mouth before he finished his furious belly slap fuck. Thank God he wore a condom. He came so hard that I could feel the heat of the condom filling with semen. This went on for another hour and a half until three of them had fucked me in the face and ass. I was exhausted.

I thanked them for the adventure and told them to email me at wakker9@yahoo.com the next time they came to town. And they did!

Lightning Source UK Ltd.
Milton Keynes UK
UKHW022016190421
382278UK00003B/629